MW00906869

3.31.2021

This book is dedicated to those who serve and protect our great country and communities

&

to Jenni Wilde Hendricks for her tireless efforts rescuing dogs.
I admire all of you.

~ Jenn

This book is dedicated to my family.
~ Chloe

January 2021

Officer

Inspired by Rachel Morris
Written by Jenn Morris
Illustrated by Chloe Mooring

I was born in a shelter. This was all
I had ever known. I was a runt. I felt
ugly. My body was awkward. I
wished someone loved me.

I was so scared. It was so loud. It was never quiet. It was cold. I sat on old newspaper. It was clean, but not sterile. I did not get let out unless my crate was being cleaned. The space was small. The bars blocked my view.

People came in all day. Sometimes they just stared at me. Sometimes they petted me. Many times, they would not even make eye contact.

There was nothing I could do. I had to sit there and wait. I wished I had a home. I wished I was loved. I wished I had a family.

The day came when everything I knew finally changed.

A man came in. He walked with determination and purpose. He stood straight. He looked honorable. He seemed brave and selfless. I could tell he was physically strong, but emotionally he was just as strong.

He looked in each puppy filled crate carefully. He stood in front of my crate. We made eye contact. I could see love, honesty, and compassion in his deep eyes. I really liked him. I felt connected to him.

Then ... It FINALLY HAPPENED!
He adopted me!
I got a FUR-EVER home!

I was just an odd-looking puppy, but I had finally been adopted!

He said I had big feet, but that I would grow into them.

He said I had sharp teeth, but he gave me toys to chew on.

He said I was silly, but he said I was very smart. He said I had potential.

This was the best day ever and the beginning of a new life for us both.

I felt great!

I felt important!

I felt loved!

People called my new 'fur-ever' owner "Officer". His name suited him so well.

Officer took such good care of me. He would run with me every day. I got so good at running I did not need a leash to keep up with my Officer.

He threw balls and toys until I was exhausted. I loved this game and we would play it for hours.

We played 'tug of war' with a rope, too. It was so fun.

He fed me healthy food and gave me fresh water every day.

My Officer was never mean. My life was perfect.

My Officer was the best owner in the world and my best friend.

My Officer trained to be ready, to adapt and to overcome all challenges in unexpected situations and environments.

I was so proud of my Officer. He was a dedicated "USMC". USMC stands for United States Marine Corps. The U.S. Marine Corps is one of the eight uniformed services of the United States.

Officer said I was "Semper Fidelis" which means "Always Faithful" to him.

Life with Officer was so good!

I loved my Officer and I was faithful to him.

One day Officer got a letter. It was a clean, white, crisp letter. The letter and envelope had red and blue stripes. It had gold stars on it, too. The letter looked very official and important.

Officer sat down and opened the letter slowly. He read the letter quietly to himself. My Officer stared at the letter a long time. He hung his head and began to softly weep.

I sat beside him. I tried to be brave for both of us.

I had never seen Officer so sad. It broke my heart.

A few days later Officer sold his car, gave away all his clothes, and donated all the household items.

Nothing was left, but .... me.

Officer put a duffle bag on the bed. The bag had a patch on it. The patch read "USMC". Officer packed the bag.

My Officer was incredibly sad. I was sad.

What was happening?

What was in that letter?

In the morning my Officer loaded the packed USMC bag into a yellow and black car. Officer put me into the car, too. I could feel the tension.

The next thing I knew we were at a place for "lost or unwanted" animals called a shelter.

I was neither. I knew who I belonged to. I belong with my Officer. I knew where I lived. I lived with my Officer.

Still, my Officer took me inside. He was sad as he filled out papers. He gave the volunteer a bag with my 'tug of war' rope, the ball he tossed for me and my food and water bowls. I was confused.

I felt his heart breaking. My heart was breaking, also. My Officer had no close family or friends. No one was there for either of us.

Officer said he had a job to do. He had made a promise to our country. My Officer said he had to keep his promise. After all, my Officer and I were "Always Faithful".

With tears in his eyes, my Officer said he would take me to the Middle East if he could, but he was not allowed. He was called for active duty and he said something about a two-year tour.

I did not understand.

What was going on?

My Officer gave me one last hug and then gave my leash to the volunteer at the shelter.

I was right back where my story started.

I still did not like this place. I was so scared, again. It was still loud. It was never quiet. It was cold. Again, I sat on old newspapers. It was clean, but not sterile. The crate was small. It felt even smaller, because I had grown. The bars blocked my view, again.

I couldn't think of anything, but my Officer. I was trying to be brave. I wanted my Officer back. I wanted to wag my tail and be happy.

I was so heartbroken.

I was "Always Faithful".

This new normal was horrible. I was losing hope, but I did not want to.

Days went by and I did not know how long I had been back in the shelter. I lost track of the days.

The paper on the outside above my small crate read "Deployed USMC". I am not sure what it means to you, but to me it meant I once belonged to my Officer. I did not belong to him anymore.

I wondered if Officer thought of me. I thought of him. I missed him. I loved him.

I had to wait again for the day to come when everything I knew changed.

Then it happened...

I saw and heard something new.

An old gray-haired man walked by my crate with a cute little girl. The man was wearing a hat. On the hat it had a patch that read "Retired USMC". I remembered seeing "USMC" on my Officer's bag!

I stood up. I felt very shy, but managed to wag my tail.

I did not want to get my hopes up, but maybe Retired USMC knew my Officer.

The Retired USMC called over a volunteer and asked if he could meet me. The volunteer took me out of my crate.

We went to a private puppy playroom, so we could get acquainted. We spent a long time together. I got to roam around the room, pounce, and act silly.

The little girl held me and cuddled me. The Retired USMC scratched my belly and rubbed my ears. I even got to sit in each of their laps.

The little girl kept asking me to do tricks and gave me commands. My Officer taught me so much. Everything the little girl asked me to do I could do it easily!

When I saw Retired USMC's hat it made me think of my Officer. I sure did miss him, but this had been a FUN day!

The little girl had a huge smile on her pretty face. I got close and licked her face. She tasted like cookies.

I love Cookies!

At the end of the play date a volunteer looked at me and said my luck had changed! The volunteer said I was going home today!!!! It FINALLY HAPPENED! I was going to my FUR-EVER home! All I kept thinking was, I am finally going to see my Officer again!!!

The car ride was great with Cookies and Retired USMC! They laughed, smiled and talked the whole trip. They even sang songs with the radio. I put my head out the window while I sat in Cookies' lap. We did not go to my Officer's home. Instead, we went to Cookies' house. I was confused, but excited.

Retired USMC and Cookies took me
to their home and introduced me to
Cookies' daddy. Cookies' daddy
seemed brave, kind, and selfless. I
could tell he was physically &
emotionally strong. He reminded me
of my Officer.

Cookies' daddy wore a shirt that read "NYPD". NYPD stands for The New York City Police Department. I learned the NYPD is known as New York's Finest; what an honor!

Cookies told me her daddy, NYPD, helped train dogs to assist police officers with their duties.

NYPD let me stay home all weekend. I played with my new toys that Retired USMC had gotten me. I got to run around outside in the back yard. NYPD threw a ball for me. I even slept in Cookies' room on her bed!

I was so happy, again. We spent a lot of quality time together.

I liked being a family with Cookies, Retired USMC, and NYPD. In fact, I loved all of them.

On Monday, NYPD woke me and Cookies up early. He said I was going to work with him.

As we rode in the car to the office, NYPD told me his mission was to 'enforce laws, preserve peace, protect the people while maintaining order'. NYPD told me I would need to be "Fidelis ad mortem". NYPD explained that meant to be "Faithful until the end". I wanted to be just like that too, faithful until the end.

At NYPD's office, I was expected to obey, which was easy because my Officer had taught me so much.

I had to follow commands without hesitation. I did it every time.

I got evaluated for running obstacle courses. I did amazing. NYPD studied my endurance levels and speed. I even got to show off my abilities on agility courses. I got to jump over walls, crawl through tubes and climb stairs. I chased people and learned to hold them down until NYPD called out for me to stop. I learned how to sniff for bombs, search for illegal drugs and assist in locating missing persons.

NYPD called it work, but for me it was FUN!

I wished my Officer could have seen me.

I loved making NYPD proud! He had a great smile. I loved going to work with NYPD.

One day a strange thing happened.

A veterinarian checked me over and said I was healthy. I went to a special dog groomer and got a bubble bath. I got my nails clipped and my teeth brushed.

Then, the most amazing thing happened! NYPD took off my old collar. He replaced my collar with a vest! The vest had NYPD on it!!

I felt so special and important!

The vest was supposed to keep me safe from bullets. I loved it! It suited me well. That afternoon there was a police ceremony.

At the police ceremony, I got a new name. I was renamed "K9 Officer"! I loved it! It was the BEST name ever!

Can you believe it? I grew up and became an Officer just like my Officer!

I was so proud of myself! I knew my Officer would be so proud of me too! I am mature, strong, brave and dependable just like my Officer and NYPD!

We all have jobs to do. We all made a promise to protect and serve. I will always keep my promises.

I admire my Officer for keeping his promise to protect our country.

I admire NYPD for being so faithful to protect citizens and community.

I will always do what I can to make them proud of me.

I understand now why my Officer left. It is the meaning of life, to have a calling and a purpose.

I am proud that MY Officer serves our country and I am proud that NYPD serves our communities. I have a job to do, too. My life is amazing. I am happy. My life has purpose.

A letter to those I love ~

Thank you, my Officer, for loving me enough to adopt me and rescue me from the shelter. I was and will always be faithful to you.

Thank you, Retired USMC, for seeing me, my potential and giving me a second chance at life.

The Few. The Proud. The Marines. Thank you for your service Sir.

Thank you, Cookies, for loving me unconditionally. Every dog should know what it feels like to be so loved, appreciated, wanted and needed. Also, you smell really good. Thank you for letting me sleep with you.

Thank you, NYPD, for trusting me, and allowing me to serve and protect beside you. I will always be faithful until the end.

Thank you, reader, for reading my story. Share my story.

With love, K9 Officer

~ The End

A lesson to learn from this story is to adopt from a shelter.

Shelter animals are perfect pets waiting on a 'fur-ever' home.

It is never the end of the story, just a new chapter ...